Arkwright the Duck

PLEASE TAKE
ME HOME
WITH YOU.

Sue Wilkins

Illustrated by Liz Furness

Cromford Mills Map

River Derwe

Scarthin Rock.

Old loom Shop.

First mill

mill Race.

Mill manager's house.

Sir Richard Arkwright of Cromford Mill fame
Now has a little duck bearing his name...

Take a look at my home from a bird's-eye view.
There's a canal, a river and railway too.

The Cromford canal is my family's home,
But I've always yearned to travel and roam.

5

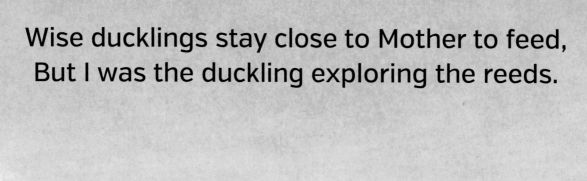

Wise ducklings stay close to Mother to feed,
But I was the duckling exploring the reeds.

While 'neath Mother's feathers, warm and dry,

I'd see water vole glide silently by...

And dragonflies darting to and fro,
Skimming the water, fast and low.

At dusk, bats flit among the trees,
While ducklings settle down to sleep.

Our bed-time story was 'The Tunnel that Roars',
A place that no duck ever went to explore.

During the night, while owls are hooting,
In the distance, a train is tooting.

The water is calm, whatever the weather,
Till the boat chugs by and ruffles my feathers.

I flap out of the way, for safety's sake,
As it leaves a huge bow wave, in its wake.

I sit on the prow and travel in style
Up and down the canal, mile after mile.

I always get lots of admiring looks
And it's fun to look down at the other ducks.

I knew I was different from all the rest,
And when the time came to leave the nest,

I waddled into the Mill Yard one day
And liked it so much, I decided to stay.

Through the Mill Yard the Mill Race flows,
That drove the water wheels, long ago.

Water should always be treated with care.
It can even give little ducks a scare.

The 'Race' has a waterfall that's called a weir,
Which a clever duck should learn to fear.

While lazily floating, I drifted too near
And before I could stop... I had disappeared.

In a flurry of feathers, swept over the top...

...'til I splashed down below with a rather loud ... **plop!**

And floated again, the right way up,
A very frightened and ruffled duck.

I was tossed about on a fast moving tide,
Through an underground tunnel, not very wide.

Battered and bruised... I could see a light.
The end of the tunnel was in sight.

And where do you think this adventure ends?
Back on the canal, amongst my friends.

And where did I finally come to rest?
Not far from home and my family's nest!

Ducklings now have a new bedtime story,
All about my brief moment of glory.

Arkwright, the very first duck to explore
The mystery of 'The Tunnel that Roars'.

Now I'm working, it's such a thrill.
I'm here to help restore the Mill.

I'm cute and fluffy, at a price you'll afford,
And live in the Mill Shop, where I can't be ignored.

Please take me on your travels, far or near,
...to see the sea from the end of a pier,

...or flying high, looking out from a plane,
And I won't ever mind if it starts to rain!

Take me on holiday, out in the sun.
Together we'll have big buckets of fun!

Now I'm a star, a mascot, no less!
It's hard to believe, I must confess.

Soon the Mill wheels will turn once more... with luck,
And a little help from Arkwright the Duck.

The End

First published in Great Britain in 2016 by

Bannister Publications Ltd
118 Saltergate
Chesterfield
Derbyshire S40 1NG

ISBN 978-1-909813-22-9

First printed in 2016; reprinted in 2017 and 2019

A catalogue record for this book is available from the British Library

Designed by Escritor Design, Chesterfield, Derbyshire
Printed and bound in Great Britain by Short Run Press Ltd, Exeter, Devon

Short Run Press places a great emphasis on environmental protection. Whether it be the sourcing of materials
from suppliers also based in the West Country, to using vegetable-based inks on press, we consider the impact
and try to do the right thing. Working with our paper merchants we have the opportunity now to
produce our books with a Carbon Neutral Footprint.
Recycling is also an important part of Short Run Press. We recycle all our waste paper and have
contracts for the safe collection and disposal of waste chemicals. The volume of waste has been
reduced significantly through our continual investment in increasingly efficient and environmentally
focused machinery. Short Run Press Ltd is certified by the Forest Stewardship Council, guaranteeing
that the paper comes from well managed forests and other controlled sources.
From the forester to consumer, we all have a responsibility to protect and sustain the natural environment.